Dear Parent:

Congratulations! Your child is taking the first steps on an exciting journey. The destination? Independent reading!

STEP INTO READING® will help your child get there. The program offers five steps to reading success. Each step includes fun stories and colorful art. There are also Step into Reading Sticker Books, Step into Reading Math Readers, Step into Reading Phonics Readers, Step into Reading Write-In Readers, and Step into Reading Phonics Boxed Sets—a complete literacy program with something for every child.

Learning to Read, Step by Step!

Ready to Read   Preschool–Kindergarten
• big type and easy words • rhyme and rhythm • picture clues
For children who know the alphabet and are eager to begin reading.

Reading with Help   Preschool–Grade 1
• basic vocabulary • short sentences • simple stories
For children who recognize familiar words and sound out new words with help.

Reading on Your Own   Grades 1–3
• engaging characters • easy-to-follow plots • popular topics
For children who are ready to read on their own.

Reading Paragraphs   Grades 2–3
• challenging vocabulary • short paragraphs • exciting stories
For newly independent readers who read simple sentences with confidence.

Ready for Chapters   Grades 2–4
• chapters • longer paragraphs • full-color art
For children who want to take the plunge into chapter books but still like colorful pictures.

STEP INTO READING® is designed to give every child a successful reading experience. The grade levels are only guides. Children can progress through the steps at their own speed, developing confidence in their reading, no matter what their grade.

Remember, a lifetime love of reading starts with a single step!

For Kevin, my favorite
travel companion —M.L.

Visit us on the Web!
StepIntoReading.com
randomhouse.com/kids

Educators and librarians, for a variety of teaching tools, visit us at RHTeachersLibrarians.com

ISBN 978-0-7364-3089-0 (trade) — ISBN 978-0-7364-8142-7 (lib. bdg.)

Printed in the United States of America
10 9 8 7 6 5 4 3 2

STEP INTO READING®

STEP 2

Travel Like a Princess

By Melissa Lagonegro

Illustrated by Francesco Legramandi
and Gabriella Matta

Random House 🏠 New York

A princess loves
to plan for a trip.
Belle reads lots
of books and maps.

She learns
about the places
she will visit.

Belle travels
to an old castle.
She uses her map
to find a secret room.

The room is filled
with books!

A princess loves
to visit new places.

Merida and Elinor travel
to a new kingdom.
They ride their horses.

A princess loves
to meet new people.

Merida and Elinor meet
another royal family.
They make new friends.

A princess loves
to try new things.

Tiana sails

on a ship

for the first time!

A princess loves
to explore other lands.

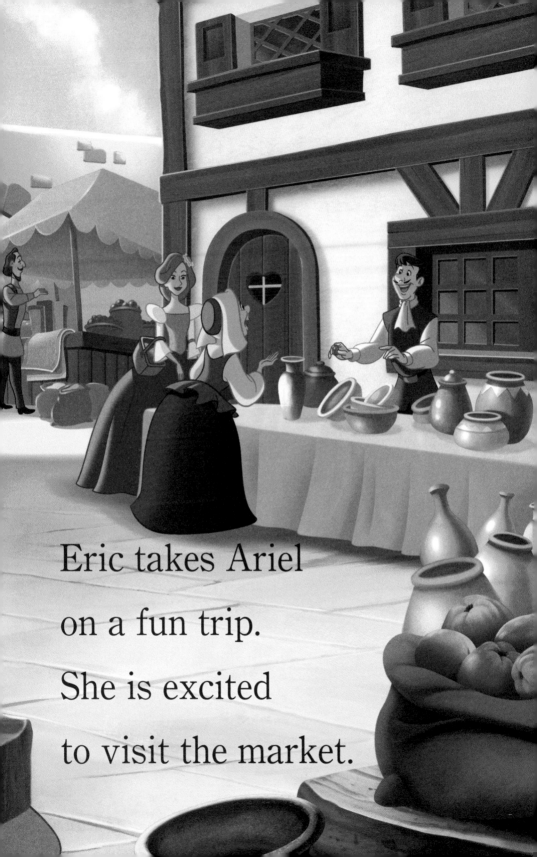

Eric takes Ariel
on a fun trip.
She is excited
to visit the market.

A princess loves
to eat new things.
Ariel and Eric try
tasty donuts.

They dance
to music.

They watch
a puppet show.

A princess loves

to have adventures.

Rapunzel and Flynn
climb a mountain
to visit friends.

Rapunzel and Flynn reach the top!

They are greeted
by their friends.

A princess loves
to bring things back
from her travels.

Cinderella gathers shells
from the beach.
She will always
remember her trip!

Where would <u>you</u> like
to visit?

© Disney

© Disney

© Disney

© Disney

© Disney

© Disney

© Disney

© Disney

© Disney

© Disney

© Disney

© Disney

© Disney

© Disney

© Disney

© Disney

© Disney

© Disney

© Disney

© Disney

© Disney

© Disney•Pixar

© Disney

© Disney

© Disney•Pixar